# Flight 725

Published by Skylar Publications

ISBN: 979-8-9904480-4-9
Cover design by Renee Wallace
Printed in the United States of America
First Edition

For permissions, inquiries, or more information, visit:
Publishing.skylarpublications@gmail.com

# TABLE OF CONTENTS

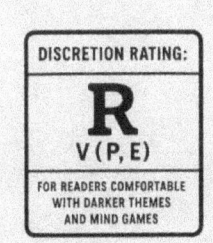

DISCRETION RATING:

**R**

V ( P, E )

FOR READERS COMFORTABLE
WITH DARKER THEMES
AND MIND GAMES

# WELCOME ABOARD FLIGHT 725

## A Journey Born from Books, Birthdays, and a Brilliant Idea

What happens when two women who share a love for storytelling, a vibrant book club community, and even the same birthday—*7/25*—decide to write together? You get Kaylynn Hunt and Octavia Grant: a dynamic duo whose creative spark took flight through EyeCU Reading & Chatting.

Their first collaboration, *Hwy 725*, debuted in 2024. That story was originally born from **Freestyle Friday**, one of many brilliant ideas dreamed up by EyeCU President Ebony Evans to spark creativity and connection among members. What began as a casual writing prompt quickly evolved into a full-blown narrative—and a writing partnership neither of them saw coming.

Now, they're back with *Flight 725*—a fast-paced, high-stakes thrill ride that proves the sky is *not* the limit. Blending suspense, secrets, and sharp storytelling, Kaylynn and Octavia invite you to buckle up for a wild ride.

This isn't just a book—it's the next leg of a journey that started with friendship, fueled by faith, fiction, and fate.

Enjoy the flight.

# PROLOGUE

"I don't like this," Tamara said hesitantly as she looked at the plane tickets that Terrence handed her.

She wanted to be grateful and appreciative for having a man who listened. For having a man that she didn't have to tell things to more than once. She loved Terrence. But she knew that for every positive thing she had to say about him, he had a negative thing to say about her. She was a pessimist, a loner, a Debbie Downer.

Terrence exhaled loudly.

"What the fuck? Yo, I'm done with this shit, T!" Terrence shouted as he threw his hands in the air. He was frustrated.

"Terrence, I-"

"Nah, I'm done with this shit Tamara. After five years of this, I'm done!"

Tears stung Tamara's eyes. She knew this outburst would come someday. Terrence was sick of her. It was obvious that he was done trying to please her. She didn't mean to be this way. The wet blanket that always seemed to smother the life out of a joyful occasion.

In casual conversation, she mentioned to Terrence that she had never been to LA. She had become a frequent flyer at the age of five. Flying domestically and internationally with her parents.

She had experienced cultures and tasted cuisines that most people had never heard of. But she had never been to the West Coast. Terrence had taken that knowledge and purchased two first-class tickets to the City of Angels and had what appeared to be a full itinerary of the things they'd do when they got there.

But still, she couldn't pretend. Tamara was a Seer, a gift passed onto her from her mother, a Gullah Geechee woman from Charleston, South Carolina. She had the ability to see and sense things that others couldn't. This was information that she had never shared with him.

So, now as she stood in her kitchen holding tickets that seemed hot enough to burn a hole in her hand, she still couldn't bring herself to explain the truth about herself to him. Instead, she simply tried to calm him down.

"Baby, I'm not-"

"You're not what, Tamara? You're not appreciative, you're not grateful, you're not thankful. For the past five years, I've tried to do everything, anything that I could think of to make you happy. But none of them are good enough for you. At this point, I'm done try-"

"Baby, no. Please don't finish that sentence," Tamara interrupted as she invaded his personal space. Placing her hand on his mouth and her head on his chest, she could feel his heart pounding against his rib cage. She could also see the things she had forced herself to forget.

Old memories, old pictures, old text messages. Correction, not old sentiments at all. No, what she saw was proof, proof that her man had begun seeing someone else behind her back. Proof that when he said he was working late, he was actually at the Budget Inn with Tiffany. His coworker, with the janky BBL and hip-length box braids.

This knowledge didn't come from her ability to see or predict things. The knowledge of his affair came from the fact that Terrence didn't realize that his iPhone and iPad were linked. She viewed every sordid detail: the pictures, the cash apps, the receipts. But nothing butchered her more than the text messages.

Seeing him professing his love to Tiffany, while badgering her name. Sharing with his side chick that she didn't appreciate him and all she did was complain. His actions and his words crushed her, but Tamara couldn't deny that it was her weird behavior that was pushing him away.

She just didn't know how to make him understand that she wasn't trying to be a wet blanket. She just had the ability to see or sense danger. So instead of telling him, she kept it to herself. And now she was at risk of losing her man.

*"Nah, that ghetto Barbie can't have my man,"* Tamara thought.

So, going against her better judgement and the spiritual gift that had never led her wrong, Tamara prepared to do damage control.

"Terrence, baby calm down. When I said I didn't like this, I meant that I didn't like that you paid for this extravagant trip by yourself. With you paying the full construction cost on our home and covering my tuition out of pocket, I would've helped pay for this trip if I'd known. I don't ever want you to wear yourself thin because of me. I'd lose it if something happened to you," Tamara admitted honestly as she kissed his lips tenderly.

She could feel the tension leaving his body.

"Well, you just make sure that once you have MD on the end of your name that you sneak me into your office and give me some brain surgeon type head," Terrence laughed.

"You are so nasty. You already know that I will," Tamara joked, but was very serious. Fellatio was her specialty, and she took pride in servicing her man. They both knew it. "Now, tell me about this trip,"

Terrence beamed like a 60-watt bulb. Pride was all over his face as he prepared to tell her everything.

"We leave on Saturday. I have us doing everything, Babe. We're having a sunset dinner in Nobu, the Hollywood Sign Hiking Trail, there are some vineyards I want us to try, and on the last day, Rodeo Drive, because my future doctor needs some new clothes and purses. I want your first trip to LA to be memorable. I love you, Baby. I'm so proud of you. If your mom and dad could see you, they'd be so proud," Terrence proclaimed.

His heart swelled with pride all over again as he watched Tamara's eyes water. Leaving her was never in the plans. He loved her too much for that. He just wanted her to be a little more optimistic and less pessimistic.

"Thank you, baby. I can't wait. Since we leave in two days, I'm going to start getting packed. Then I'm going to take a hot shower. Join me before you go to work," Tamara said as she sensually stroked his already hard third leg.

"You don't have to tell me twice," Terrence smirked.

No more words needed to be spoken. Tamara smiled devilishly, but on the inside her stomach was in knots. Though she had never been to Los Angeles, she truly didn't want to go on this trip. But for Terrence, she'd grin and bear it.

"Guide my steps, God. Something does not feel right," Tamara said anxiously, as she walked into her room and prepared to pack for her trip aboard Flight 725.

# Flight 725

# CHAPTER 1

"Good luck. Even though you don't need it. I know you got this," Phoenix said as she released Julius.

"Thank you, baby. I'm going to miss you. I'll make sure to call you when I land."

"That job is yours," she said before placing a parting peck on his lips.

"I love you. You know that?" Julius said.

"Love you too," Phoenix responded as Julius walked away.

Phoenix watched Julius walk into the airport terminal with heaviness in her heart. For some reason, she felt as if this would be the last time she'd see him. It hurt but not as much as it should've. She noted that. There was a numbness that had crept up and she wondered if it was because of the third or fifth time she'd caught him cheating.

The first time she forgave him, believing his explanation of being afraid to love her fully because he'd been hurt in the past. She was convinced by his tears, his pleading for a chance to love her properly. By the fifth time, she really didn't care what he had to say. Did she know she deserved better? Of course. But letting go was easier said than done.

Julius had been there for her when she needed him in many ways. When her sister overdosed, he held her at night when she cried. The time her car was stolen, Julius was there to be her transportation until she found some of her own. In those trying times, he was her crutch. It was because of that; she hung on for so long. Phoenix felt like she owed it to him. But she didn't; she owed something to herself.

She loved him, was in love with him at one point. As she looked at him feeling nothing, she wondered if that was still the case. The feeling she used to get being around him, the giddiness, the awe, had been replaced with a sense of familiarity. In that moment, she realized she was only clinging to comfort. As she watched him turn to take one last look at her, she smiled, waved and knew that was it for them.

Julius made his way to the gate. Phoenix's voice kept echoing in his head. 'You only love the idea of me.' That's what she'd told him on the ride to the airport. What exactly did she mean by that? Was she right?

He was lucky to have her, he knew that. She was beautiful, caring, sweet and loyal. Phoenix lit up rooms when she walked into them. Julius knew he couldn't let a person like her go. But was she right? Was it just the idea of having her in his corner? Did he really love her?

How could he and constantly let her down, break her heart? How could he keep betraying her? These were the thoughts running through his mind as he arrived at his departure gate. When he found a seat, he pulled out his cell.

"Hey babe, I'm at the gate."

"Cool. What time do you land?" The melodic voice on the other end questioned.

"It's at like midnight, I think."

"I'll check the flight status. What's the flight number again?"

"Flight 725."

"Ok. I can't wait to see you."

"Me either, I'll be there in a few hours, love."

"I love you."

"Love you too."

Julius disconnected the call then scoped the other passengers in the area as he found some music to listen to. There were a few ladies that caught his eye.

He noticed this one woman who looked to be his speed, but she was with her dude. She didn't look happy with him, though. She looked familiar. There was another he would make sure to flirt with, she seemed preoccupied as she looked at the screen of her tablet.

Julius wondered how full the flight was about to be. After scrolling through a few of his contacts, sending off text messages letting his women know he was headed out of town for work, he settled into the music playing through his earbuds.

*Attention passengers of Maahes Flight 725 to LAX. My name is Annisa On behalf of the airline, we thank you for choosing Maahes Air. In just a few moments, we will begin boarding at Gate D12. Please have your boarding passes ready. We will board by group number, board with your group. I now invite those with small children or passengers that require special assistance to the gate at this time.*

Harold began gathering his things. He was in group two, he wanted to be prepared. Being the first in line wasn't his style but he considered it. It was still hard for him to believe he'd won this trip. Once he was on the flight, they wouldn't be able to take it back.

Initially, Harold thought it had been a mistake or a joke one of his friends decided to play. The contest he was informed of winning, he was still trying to figure out when he'd entered. The more he questioned the woman on the phone about details and figured out they weren't trying to get money from him. They'd even booked the flight for him, given him a choice of hotels and made all the arrangements. Harold hadn't ever won a thing, this felt like a grand prize. There was no way he'd turn down a free trip.

L.A. would be right on time. The deal he'd been working on just closed. This would be the perfect celebration. All the apprehension he'd had at first had dissipated once he verified the reservations. Harold no longer cared how he got entered into the contest, he'd won. He was about to live it to the fullest. He'd already put in a search on the 'hook up' app for the area. Harold's mind was already in party mode. He was ready to make a movie.

Clarissa couldn't wait to board. She'd been sitting at the bar a few feet away from the gate. When she heard the announcement for pre-boarding, she stumbled over to a seat near the gate. Before flopping down in the seat, she noted the guy in the row of seats checking her out. He was fine based on the quick glance she afforded him. Now sitting a few seats over from him, she looked more closely. There was ruggedness about his demeanor. She liked that. Mischievous thoughts began churning in her mind. He could be something for her to do while in L.A.

It had been years since she'd graced the city of angels with her presence. The last time still only came to her in flashes of memory. Though the details are fuzzy, it had been life changing.

"I should've been with you."

"Excuse me?" Clarissa responded.

"At the bar. That's where you were, right? I should've been with you, getting the party started."

Clarissa giggled.

"Is it that obvious?"

"I mean," he shrugged. "Not really but your eyes are a little glassy."

"Tell me you've been checking me out without telling me you've been checking me out."

"Ha! Maybe I was. Is that a crime?"

"I don't know. Would your wife think it was?"

"Probably, if I had one. I'm Harold." He outstretched his hand.

"Clarissa." She placed hers in his. "But you can call me Rissa."

"What takes you to Los Angeles, Rissa?"

"A role."

"You're an actress. That tracks, you're beautiful."

"Thank you."

"What's the movie about?"

"It's about a girl that lost her sister after a wild night of partying."

"Wow! Sounds interesting."

"It will be. It'll be my first lead."

"Congratulations."

"Thank you."

"That is call for celebration. Will you share a drink with me when we board?"

"Uh sure, but you don't even know if we're sitting close to each other."

"It doesn't matter."

"Smooth, Hank, smooth."

"Harold," he corrected.

"I know but Hank suits you better. I'm calling you Hank."

*"I told your ass not to be dragging. You almost had us miss the flight."*

Hank looked up at the guy that had just walked by with a woman scurrying behind him. They took a seat across from where he and Rissa were seated.

*Attention passengers for Maahes Flight 725 to Los Angeles. We welcome passengers in group two to begin boarding at this time.*

"That's me," Harold stated.

"Me too," Clarissa responded as she stood.

"No shit. Let me help you with that," he said, taking the handle of her rollaway carryon.

*"You see they're already boarding. You're lucky we weren't any later."*

Shania sat in a seat near the window with her back to the tarmac. She observed everyone as they prepared to board. But it was the couple she'd given the most scrutiny. The demeanor of the woman screamed fear and the man she was with was the cause of it. Of that, Shania was certain. Most of the other people around her seemed excited or joyful about getting on this plane. But that woman just didn't. Maybe she had a fear of flying but Shania felt as if it were him she was more afraid of. There were a few others that didn't seem so jovial that caught her attention. But they were traveling alone. It was something about that couple that had her senses tingling.

After waiting for everyone to board, she finally rose from her seat then strolled to the gate. It was in her nature to observe. Her career as a criminal profiler only amplified this inherent habit. As she made her way down the jetway Shania chuckled to herself. Before she knew it her mind was churning with things she'd do to the abusive guy and how she might get away with it on the flight. She shook her head trying to rid her mind of the thoughts.

# CHAPTER 2

**The night before...**

"I know you have been seeing that bitch."

Carlos sighed.

"I haven't been seeing anyone. I work, Franessa. You know that thing that lets me afford all this," he said as he threw his hands in the air.

She knew he was frustrated with her when he used her full name. He only called her by the stupid name when he was pissed. But she didn't care, her head and heart were telling her something wasn't right.

"It doesn't take days at a time."

"It does if I fly a plane. The same thing I've been doing since we met, since we were engaged, and since we got married."

"You used to take me with you on long trips."

"Franessa, not every trip. Is that what this is about? You want to go on a trip? Just fucking say that."

Carlos took a drink of the cognac in his hand. He hated it when she got like this. Everything she said, thought, expressed was over the top and unreasonable. He wasn't sure where she hid all the jealousy and insecurity when they were dating but he wanted her to put it back. They had only been married for two years and things were getting progressively worse.

Usually, he played into her antics giving her extra reassurance and attention. But today he wasn't feeling it, he was tired of it. Carlos loved his wife with everything he had. But it was days like this when he felt like anything he did for her was in vain.

She got the house she wanted even though it was way over the budget he had set for them. The car she drove, luxurious. He surprised her with gifts. And honestly, all he did was work. He didn't have time to do the cheating she accused him of. Well, he didn't have the energy to do the cheating she accused him of. There were plenty of flight attendants that he could occupy his travel time with. But he never had.

"I don't want to go to L.A."

"What do you want, Nessa?"

"You!"

"I'm right here."

"Until tomorrow, then you're gone again."

"Come with me to L.A."

"Ugh!"

"Then I guess it's not me you want. You just want to complain. If you wanted me, L.A. would be just fine."

She was silent. Carlos stared at the side of her head. She'd averted his gaze.

Carlos drained what was left in his glass without ever taking his eyes from her. The thoughts churning in his head were getting darker by the second. He didn't need the headaches she brought on. He didn't need to drink as much as he was the day before he was due to fly but he still stood and poured another.

When Franessa met Carlos, she was working at a high-end boutique as a salesperson. He was walking through the mall and ran into her while she was on her lunch break, literally. Her first response was set to be a string of profanities until she looked up. His grey eyes stalled her words. Carlos apologized profusely, she didn't even hear him, she was so mesmerized by his looks. His offer to take her to dinner as an apology felt as if she'd won the lottery.

After a few dates, she thought that Carlos was her dream come true. He was caring, funny, he catered to her. It was what she needed. Because Julius had turned her life inside out. She thought he loved her. But he proved not to be the man she thought he was. Carlos came along right on time. And everything he said or did made her feel cherished, beautiful, and loved. But nothing could make her feel worthy.

Nessa thought that getting the things she dreamed of would make her happy. But the dream house, the car, all the clothes in her closet still left her lonely. When Carlos wasn't there, thoughts of Julius seeped to the surface. None of those things she had could stop the yearning she still felt for him.

She didn't know how to function in a space that didn't have chaos. She grew up with it and lived in it her whole life. She was trying, she really was. Knowing the way Carlos actually loved her; she wanted to make it work with him. But all that just fueled her fear of losing him and the cycle started all over again.

"Baby, I'm sorry. You are right. I'll go to L.A. with you."

"I'll arrange it, I'm going to bed."

Carlos wanted to show more joy with her declaration, but his spirit had been disturbed. It was going to take some time for him to settle his soul. He wanted her to marinate in her thoughts. She was the one causing discourse. When he slid between the sheets of their king-sized bed, he told himself, his mood would be better in the morning. Then fell into slumber thinking about what things they could do in L.A. that would get his wife back to the woman he loved.

When her husband made his way to bed, Franessa sat reflecting. One thing Franessa was grateful for was the way Carlos handled her outbursts. Even when he got so frustrated with her that he raised his voice, she loved him for it.

Because the household that she was caged in from a child to pre-teen was much more volatile. She remembered sleeping in a closet to hide from the wrath of her father. Her past was something she never talked about. It was a thing she wanted to forget.

Carlos had no idea the things she'd endured. In her mind if he had, he wouldn't want her. She'd told him her parents were deceased when they met. She never expected their dinner to ever grow into a marriage. But there was no way her husband could ever meet her mother, he would run. One look at her track marked arms and sunken eyes and Carlos would turn tails on her. Why would he want a woman who could potentially end up looking like that?

Even though Nessa hadn't touched any drug a day in her life, all her thoughts had validity as far as she was concerned. The same thoughts that told her Carlos would cheat on her. The brain that created those thoughts told her to smell his underwear when she pulled them out of the laundry. The same brain had her following him when he said he was going to the gym. It was the same brain that wouldn't allow her to enjoy the life she had for fear of losing it.

Nessa wouldn't listen to that same brain when it tried to tell her she was the one that would drive him away. When it told her maybe she should enjoy what she had. She didn't listen when it told her not to drug his food, so he'd fall asleep and stay home. She would just watch him sleep. She told herself she was not the cause of their problems no matter what Carlos or her brain told her in that regard.

Before she joined him in bed, she packed a bag. She would go to L.A. with him. She wasn't ever letting him out of her sight.

# CHAPTER 3

"I told your ass not to be dragging. You almost had us miss the flight. Can you stop looking so scared? You're out here looking like I be whooping your ass," Terrence joked as he and Tamara took their seats.

He was slightly annoyed by her behavior. When he was booking the trip with the travel agent, he had expected to see the largest smile gracing Tamara's face. He knew how important it was for her to visit the West Coast. He had watched her Google things to do in Los Angeles several times, he'd even seen her reading the Los Angeles Wikipedia page just to learn the history of the city.

Tamara's behavior was unusual even for her. He hadn't expected her to be so fidgety and absent-minded. He hadn't expected her to lie about calling an Uber to take them to the airport, and he hadn't expected her to act as if she was terrified. They flew so much that they joked about purchasing their own private plane. He knew that she wasn't afraid of flying, so her behavior made no sense to him.

It filled him with pride in being able to plan a spur of the moment trip for her. He hated to compare the two, but had he secured a trip like this for Tiffany, he'd probably have to wear some type of medieval chastity device to keep her off his dick. Tiffany knew how to show a man that she appreciated him.

"Then maybe you should've brought Tiffany,"

Terrence froze in place.

"What did you say?" Terrence asked in complete shock as he nearly shit himself.

His heart slammed against his rib cage as if it were trying to break free from his chest. Tiffany had been on his mind, but he knew for a fact that he had not spoken her name.

His loud screech pulled Tamara out of the mental hell that she was momentarily in. She hadn't heard anything that he said prior to him asking her what she said.

"What?" Tamara asked as she looked around nervously.

"You said, then maybe I should've brought Tiffany. Who is that?" Terrence asked. Voice trembling.

There was no way, or at least he thought, that Tamara knew about Tiffany. He had been so careful about protecting his home life from what he deemed his personal business. He had never felt nervous or fearful around Tamara. But hearing her recite thoughts that he didn't speak, had him scared and uncomfortable.

Tamara's stomach dropped. She was so flustered that she didn't realize that she said anything. She had heard herself speaking but hadn't truly comprehended what she was saying. The look of fear on Terrence's face was almost as if he believed that she had read his mind. Yes, she had special abilities, but reading minds was not one of them.

No, what she had done was absent-mindedly spoken her own thoughts aloud. Tamara had no way of knowing that her scary behavior had some very dangerous eyes on Terrence. She had no way of knowing that Terrence was now being looked at as an enemy and threat to her. It would've been wise for her to tell him exactly what was on her mind, but since she had no clue that she was being viewed as a damsel in distress, she didn't.

At the moment she was too focused on her own thoughts. She hated to admit it, but in this instant, she would've preferred Terrence's side bitch take her place. She was never the type of woman to broach topics about another bitch, so she did what any secure woman would do. She lied.

"Excuse me? I did not say, then maybe you should've brought Tiffany. I said my head is pounding. It feels like someone beating a Timpani. So, who the fuck is Tiffany and why do you look like a deer caught in the headlights?"

Tamara had always been quick on her toes. She was blessed with the gift of gab and was quite skilled at talking herself out of any situation. Though she didn't like the idea of having to gaslight her fiancé, at this very moment, it was necessary. The look of confusion that now graced Terrence's face let her know that her quick lie and faux attitude had done exactly what she needed it to do; confused his brain enough to drop the subject.

*"Oh shit. I gotta get Tiffany off my brain,"* He thought as he stared at the fury on Tamara's face.

"I just…never mind," Terrence sighed.

"Never mind then," Tamara sucked her teeth and crossed her arms over her breast.

"Tee, what's up? We practically live on a plane or a train when I'm not working and when you don't have school. Traveling has always been the one thing that we never have disagreements about. So, why are you acting like this? What's going on for real?"

The sincerity and genuine concern in Terrence's voice nearly broke her.

"Babe, I don't think we should be on this flight. Something is going to happen on this flight that's going to damage all of us. I was born with a gift that allows me to see things. There is someone very dangerous on this plane. We need to get the fuck off Flight 725," This is what Tamara wanted to say.

She knew that Terrence deserved the truth. He deserved to know why she was so jittery and agitated, but she couldn't work up the courage to tell him. Julius, the guy she dated ten years ago, the man that was supposed to be her husband, left her because of her gift. When she warned him about seeing him involved in a car accident, he had laughed her visions off and called her crazy.

When he was involved in an accident two days later. A fatal accident that decapitated his passenger, the woman that he had been cheating on Tamara with. He called Tamara a demon and a witch and accused her of tampering with his car.

Julius had broken up with Tamara and sued her because he believed that she either tampered with his car or hired someone to do it. Once she was cleared, and the person that had tampered with his car, the deceased woman's husband, was found, Julius had tried to apologize and reconcile, but Tamara was done.

She vowed that day to never tell another living soul about her secret. Terrence was the first man that she had dated seriously since breaking up with Julius ten years ago. She didn't want to scare him off. So, saying what was truly on her mind would never happen. Instead, she focused on a different truth.

"I'm just not feeling well. And on top of that, did you see the pilot? He looks like he's under the influence of something heavy or like he hasn't had enough sleep. We've flown with this pilot several times and he's always vibrant and upbeat. He looks completely out of it. Who the fuck is he trying to be William "Whip" Whitaker? I'm just a little uncomfortable," Tamara admitted truthfully.

Terrence wanted to laugh at the reference to Denzel Washington's character in the 2012 movie Flight. But he couldn't. When he saw the pilot, he wanted to ask for a refund on the tickets. His bloodshot eyes, pale skin, and wrinkled uniform screamed substance abuse. Instead of laughing, he sighed.

"Tee, the flight is only a few hours long. What's the worst thing that could happen?"

# CHAPTER 4

*What's the worst thing that could happen?*

Tamara looked at Terrence as if he had two heads. It had to be the dumbest question that he ever asked. A lot could happen in a few hours. A lot could happen in a mere sixty seconds. Planes were literally falling out of the sky, going missing midflight, or flying into buildings. The possibilities of what the worst thing could be were endless.

"I think I need a drink or maybe something for anxiety."

It was this statement that made the hackles on the back of Terrence's neck stand. Tamara had been prescribed Xanax, but she rarely took her pills due to feeling lethargic. According to her, it left her in a zombie-like state of mind. The fact that she now wanted to take the medication disturbed him.

"Tee, can you just tell me what's really going on? It feels like you're keeping secrets."

*"Nothing good ever came from keeping secrets."*

Tamara could hear her mother's voice speaking clearly as if she were standing directly beside her. She looked around as if she were expecting to see her, but she knew that was impossible. Her mother's sentiments were right. She was always right. Secrets were the reason she was no longer here.

Her husband's secret. His Nineteen-year-old archeological student and his secret lover had gone to her parents' home demanding an explanation for why he ended their affair. When Tamara's mother answered the door, the unhinged teen fired a single round in her mother's chest before fleeing the scene. Her mother's dying words were, *"I knew she was coming."*

Anger, resentment, and grief made Tamara lash out at her father. She blamed him for her mother's death. She had gone as far as calling him a pedophile for having sex with a girl the same age as she was. Someone thirty years his junior. Her mother had always preached forgiveness, but that was not something she could do. Her death was avoidable if her father had just been a decent man. Her mother, Bella, had truly been her best friend, without her, she felt lost.

The immense guilt had crippled Dr. Dale Dennis. He had only seen his student's beauty. He had ignored the rumors of how bad her home life had been growing up. The attention she gave him made him ignore her unhinged and unstable behavior. Because of that, he had lost everything. After attending his wife's funeral, Dr. Dennis committed suicide. Tamara did not attend his funeral.

"I need to go to the restroom. I'll be right back," Tamara said as she stood to walk down the aisle. She opted for the one in the back since the one near their first-class seats was occupied.

The tremble in her voice stunned Terrence. He wanted to go after her, but he could tell that she truly needed a moment to herself. As if a spring was loaded in his back, Terrence shot up with excitement. The last time Tamara behaved this oddly, she was pregnant. Unfortunately, the pregnancy ended as a result of preterm labor. But during that time, they were the happiest they'd ever been.

*"Let it be a boy,"* Terrence thought excitedly as he waited for Tamara to return.

Julius eyes nearly ran from his head when he got a glimpse of the woman walking down the aisle. When he arrived at the airport, he saw her and thought that she was his type, but the sadness that covered her face made her unrecognizable. Now that she was a mere ten feet away from him, he could clearly see who the woman was.

He hadn't seen her in over a decade, nor did he think of her. There were too many women parading in and out of his life to dwell on the past. But as she got closer, his body reacted in a way that it hadn't in years. Before he had time to think about what he was doing, her name was out of his mouth.

"Tam?"

Tamara stopped mid-step when she heard her old nickname. Her muscles stiffened as if she were in full rigor. Everyone referred to her as Tee. Besides her deceased parents, only one other person called her Tam. Turning her head slightly to the right, Tamara nearly fainted.

"Julius, I-"

Tamara's words became lodged in her throat. She hadn't expected to see anyone she knew on this flight. And after ten years, she hadn't expected to see him.

*"This has to be a bad omen,"* She thought as she stared at the genuine smile on her ex-fiancé's face.

"I wasn't expecting to see you after all these years. You really look beautiful, Tam. Is your flight to LA business or pleasure?" Julius asked as he openly and shamelessly admired Tamara's curvy body.

His heart slammed against his chest when he saw the large curve on her ring finger. He couldn't understand why, but the sight of the engagement ring made his stomach tighten. Jealousy and anger invaded every orifice of his body, and he couldn't understand why.

Tamara could feel the heat oozing from his body. He had always been the type to think that he could put a person down then pick them up whenever he wanted to. He had expected her to just fall into place like nothing had happened, even after ten years. She could tell that nothing with him had changed. Julius was still as charming as a king cobra.

"I'm on this flight to see a man about a horse. Enjoy your flight, Julius," Tamara said sweetly before she dashed to the restroom. Her nervous system was sending warning signals through her entire body. She knew it was best to get away from him.

Julius' manhood grew three times its normal size. He hadn't seen her in years, but it was obvious that Tamara still had that same sensual hold on him. Anytime she spoke in euphemisms, it drove him insane. Though Tamara was from the city, she possessed a lot of her mother's down south mannerisms. He had always loved that about her.

He hated that he was the cause of their breaking up, but now that he had seen her again, he knew that he had to slide inside of her and apologize for all the things he had gotten wrong. He didn't care that she was on the flight with her man, she was his first. Standing up, Julius adjusted himself, stepped out of his seat and walked towards the restroom. He had joined the mile high club years ago, and now it was time he added his ex to the club as well.

"Oh my God Julius!"

Looking into the face of Franessa, the erection that was leading Julius down the aisle went limp. She was someone that he never wanted to lay eyes on again.

"What the…Aahhh!!" Julius and all the passengers screamed when a bright white light filled the plane.

# CHAPTER 5

*Bling, Bom, Boop*

The chime of the intercom sounded.

*"Good evening, folks. This is your captain speaking. Nothing too much to worry about. We just got a bit of lightning. But please remain seated until the seatbelt signs have been turned off. Our Flight time is currently three hours and thirty-nine minutes."*

He paused as if he was thinking of what to say next then continued speaking.

*"We do have a bit of weather ahead of us. To ensure everyone's safety, that seatbelt sign might be on the duration of our flight."*

Franessa stood listening to her husband's voice while staring in her lover's face. At least that's what he used to be to her.

"What are you doing here?" Julius spat with disdain.

"What anyone else does on an airplane, traveling."

She stood blocking his path, shooting metaphorical daggers at him with her eyes. The look on his face made her feel embarrassed for still wanting him.

Julius looked past her, hoping Tamara didn't come out of the restroom anytime soon.

"If you'd excuse me. I have business to take care of."

He pushed past her and left her standing in the aisle without a second look. Just as he reached the back of the plane, Tamara was exiting the restroom.

"There you are. I was coming to see if you needed assistance," Julius said in a low tone.

He pressed his body against her, blocking her path.

"I'm all set. And even if I did, I wouldn't need your help. Please get out of my way Julius."

"Don't be like that, Tam."

He leaned into her while attempting to tuck her hair behind her ear. But she slapped his hand away.

"DON'T fucking touch me," she said through gritted teeth.

Tamara didn't want to cause a scene. She didn't want to draw attention and more importantly, she didn't want Terrence to be alerted. That wouldn't be good.

Julius saw a sparkle when her hand connected with his. He caught her hand and held it.

"Oh Shit! Is that what I think it is?"

He asked as if he hadn't noticed it moments ago.

"An engagement ring, yes. Now, move around."

Julius didn't move, though; he stared at her.

"Excuse me," a woman's voice interrupted from behind.

It caught Julius off guard, he stepped aside as he turned. Tamara took the opportunity to slide by. She looked the woman in the face, silently thanking her for the interruption.

"I apologize, beautiful."

Julius ogled the gorgeous woman in front of him. Her mocha skin had a glow, something about her screamed confidence and seduction all at once. Absently, he licked his lips.

Shania rolled her eyes as she walked into the restroom. Once she closed the door, she looked at herself in the mirror.

*Calm down, that's not what you're here for.* She told herself. Because what she really wanted to do was chop him in the throat and crush his windpipe.

There was really no need for her to use the facilities. She had heard the exchange between the two of them and wanted to intervene. Boy, what she wouldn't give to be able to meet that guy on the street. Shania waited a few more seconds before washing her hands.

She hoped he'd gone back to his seat as she unlatched the door. Luckily, he had. Lucky for him, anyway.

~~~

"What took you so long? Stomach upset?" Terrence questioned once Tamara was seated.

"No. Ugg, there was a line."

As soon as the lie left her lips, she wished it hadn't. She didn't have anything to be deceptive about.

"I thought I was going to have to come get you," he chuckled.

But all she could think was how that wouldn't have gone well at all.

*Bling, Bom, Boop*

*"If we have any medical professionals on this flight please hit your call button."*

"I wonder what that's about?" Tamara stated.

She couldn't help the eerie feeling that crept up her neck. Worries of Julius were chased away by that gnawing angst she'd been trying to rid herself of all morning. It was obvious to her; her fears were coming to fruition.

Tamara noted which call lights went on, following the activities of the flight attendant when her eyes met with a woman seated a few rows up. They seemed to be glaring at her with disdain. Tamara glanced over her shoulder thinking maybe the woman was looking past her. But when she turned back the woman had averted her gaze.

*What the fuck was that about?*

# CHAPTER 6

Shania was watching everything going on from the time the flight attendant came over the intercom requesting a medical professional. A few lights went on, one of the attendants or another went to each person asking questions. She assumed they were assessing what type of doctor or nurse or whatever they were. What she also observed was the exchange with the air marshal and him going into motion.

Whatever happened appeared to be at the front of the plane, maybe first class. She was seated at the back. Not many people like being on the back of the plane but it was Shania's seat of choice. It gave her the vantage point of seeing everything going on. From her aisle seat, she saw the doctor kneeling. It looked like she was checking someone's pulse. Then the doctor or whoever they were said something to the flight attendant then she moved to the marshal.

Now, the doctor, marshal and attendant were standing at the front of the plane conversing and Shania hated she couldn't hear what they were saying. She could read faces and if it weren't for the angle of their stance and her distance, she may have been able to read some lips.

The flight wasn't completely full, but it wasn't empty either. There were enough people to be in every row but not every seat was filled. The seating floated to the front of Shania's mind because she had already begun charting her next steps. She was an overthinker, a million things went through her head at once. It was one of the things that made her good at what she did.

And just like she thought, she watched the attendant go to a few passengers then they started moving.

*Someone was dead.* They were isolating the person. Who would want to be sitting in proximity to a dead person. And the fact that they couldn't or wouldn't move the corpse let her know something was suspicious.

When the marshal went to the cockpit, she decided she needed to be more on the inside than guessing on the outside. So, she dug in her bag then headed towards the front of the plane. As soon as she stood there was a loud rumbling followed by another bright flash of light. The storm they were flying through seemed to be getting worse. If it weren't for the thunder and lightning it would be evident by the turbulence.

"Ma'am please return to your seat," one of the flight attendants told Shania.

She flashed her badge. The woman nodded then stepped aside. As Shania tried keeping her balance while holding on to the back of any seats she could, she noticed one passenger in tears while another consoled her. She also took a glance at the passenger who appeared to be asleep in the row alone. Once she reached the front area just outside the cockpit, the marshal was stepping into the area.

"I came to offer my services if needed," she said, showing him her badge.

"Thompson," he stated, extending his hand.

"Shania Brindle," she responded. "What do we have going on?"

"Deceased in row six. The surrounding passengers have been moved. Cause, yet to be determined. But given age, it's not leaning toward natural."

"Are we diverting?"

"No. The weather is worse behind and to the south than it is ahead of us. We'll proceed to our destination and go from there."

"Mind if I take a look?"

"Unless you got a mobile lab, I don't see what answers you can gather. But have at it."

Shania turned to look at the cabin. From this view, she could see all the faces, their expressions, furrowed brows. And she inconspicuously looked for traces of emotions, fear, apprehension. She didn't spend too much time looking at the body, nor did she touch him. But she did remember seeing him in the terminal area. He'd been chatting it up with a girl who stumbled over just before they'd boarded.

"Did you notice that smell?" Shania questioned Thompson as he walked up next to her.

"What smell?"

"It's a faint almond smell."

"Like the nut? I don't know if I even know what an almond smells like."

Shania gave a slight smile.

"That's fair. But it is also what cyanide poisoning smells like."

"Cyanide? I'm sorry. Are you an investigator or…" he dragged the last letter of his question out waiting for her answer.

"Apologies, I'm a profiler. I'm headed to L.A. to speak at a conference. Generally, there'd be other symptoms prior to death. Was anyone sitting next to him? Did he drink anything? Has anything been moved?"

"Gina will be able to help you with that."

Thompson motioned for Gina to come over to us.

"Hi, Gina. My name is Shania," she flashed her badge again. "Can you tell me if anything was moved from over here; what he may have had to eat or drink and whether there was anyone with him?"

"Nothing was moved."

"Good. Don't touch anything."

"There was a woman sitting next to him, but they weren't together. She had actually switched seats to sit next to him. It seemed like they'd just met. We've moved her back to her original seat. She's really upset."

"I'm going to need to speak with her. I'd rather do it away from the other passengers. Can you get her to come up this way?"

Gina nodded then headed down the aisle a few rows.

"Should we cover him up?" Thompson questioned.

"It won't hurt. Just don't touch him." Shania shrugged.

The body didn't bother her, her eyes lingered a bit longer, noticing how rosy his dark cheeks looked.

*Definitely cyanide.*

Gina returned with the teary-eyed young lady. It was the same woman she'd seen him chatting it up with before they came aboard.

"This is Clarissa," Gina introduced.

"Hello Clarissa, I'm Shania. I was wondering if I could ask you a few questions. I know this is difficult."

Clarissa nodded.

"Have you known…" Shania paused. She didn't know his name.

"Harold," Gina interjected.

"Have you known Harold long?"

Clarissa shook her head.

"Can you tell me what happened?"

"We had a couple drinks," she said on a shaky breath. "We were just talking and then he started shaking."

That was all she got out before she erupted in sobs. Gina rubbed her back to comfort her. Shania knew she wasn't going to get much more out of her. She struggled not to roll her eyes at the dramatics. She had gotten what she needed from Clarissa anyway.

"Clarissa, are you alright with Xanax? I can give you one to help calm your nerves."

Clarissa nodded.

"Gina, my bag is back at my seat. You'll find a prescription bottle in the outer pocket. If you could, please."

"Sure."

"What now?" Thompson questioned.

"Like you said, without a mobile lab, there's no way to be 100% sure. But I'm almost willing to bet a kidney he was poisoned."

"How are you so sure?"

"The almond smell, the red skin and the seizure Clarissa described are all signs of cyanide poisoning."

"When? How? Why?"

"Those are all questions that need to be answered but there's one even more important."

"What's that?"

"Who's next?"

# CHAPTER 7

With all the different people on the plane: Air Marshals, FBI Profilers, and dead passengers, the only person Franessa could focus on was the woman that had Julius' attention.

She hadn't meant to constantly turn around and glare at her, but she couldn't understand why Julius had given the woman so much attention. She couldn't deny that the woman was beautiful. In all actuality, exotic would have been a better word. Her looks alone had Franessa ready to blow a gasket.

Deep cocoa brown skin, hypnotizing light brown eyes, and slick back ponytail with loose strands hung near her ear. Her low-maintenance 'do highlighted her natural long lashes, high cheekbones, and full lips. Franessa gripped the armrest and gritted her teeth as rage overtook her. Images of Julius and the woman rolling around in a bed, naked, and sweating from the animalistic sex that Julius loved, threatened to push her over the edge.

"Who is that bitch? Is she someone that Julius was fucking with when he was with me? This is something Julius would do. Flaunt his whore in my face and expect me not to react. I bet they're having a good laugh about this. Everything I do, I do because of Julius. Drugging my husband before a coast-to-coast flight just so he couldn't leave me. Julius will never change," Franessa thought as faux images of Julius and the mystery woman continued to run rampant in her head.

She had no way of knowing that Tamara and Julius had been a couple a decade ago. But even if someone had explained that to her, she wouldn't have believed it. Once an idea formed in her head, there was no changing it. It was that very thing that made Julius leave her. Yes, he was guilty of lying and cheating, but Franessa didn't know that he was intentionally being reckless. He wanted to get caught. Doing things, hoping it would make her leave.

She refused to acknowledge that her mood swings, constant nagging, and badgering was a huge problem. She preferred to be the victim in the situations that she caused. The incident that led to Julius breaking his lease and moving in the middle of the night was Franessa setting up a birthday threesome. He was shocked when he came home and saw Franessa there with another woman.

He knew how she could be, so even though he enjoyed multiple partners, he wouldn't have ever asked for such a gift. During the encounter, Franessa became enraged. She accused Julius of being too touchy with the other woman and accused them of having an affair behind her back. Franessa tried to strangle the woman with the cord from the tableside lamp. Her antics were just too much. Julius turned his key into the leasing office and never looked back.

"Sweetheart, are you okay? You're gripping the armrest so tight. I know it's scary on the plane at the moment, but-"

"Mind your business bitch," Franessa said to the passenger, as she turned back to glare at Tamara.

"The fuck? Do you know that woman?" Terrence asked as he watched the woman glare at Tamara. He could feel the heat from her glare as he stared daggers at her.

"Nah, I don't know her," Tamara admitted as she stared back at the woman. She refused to let anyone stare her down. She was no coward. And if a staring match was what the woman wanted, she could certainly have it. As if they were true enemies, the woman rolled her eyes and sucked her teeth.

"What was that about?" Terrence asked clearly confused.

As if a light bulb had gone off in her head, Tamara smirked. The only time women hated other women they didn't even know was because of a man. She had only encountered one man from the time she got up to go to the restroom. It was truly a small world what were the odds of her, her ex, and her ex's possible ex ending up on the same plane?

"He still has women seeping out of his pores," Tamara smirked while shaking her head. The woman had no need to worry about her because Julius wasn't on her radar anymore.

"Why didn't you turn on your call light when they asked for medical professionals?"

"Because I'm not a medical professional. I'm a medical student. There's a difference. And besides, I heard the lady say there was an almond smell, which normally means cyanide poisoning. That's out of my realm of expertise. I'd rather the professionals handle whatever it is that's going on. The weather, the dead man, and any other unforeseen situations have me ready to get off this plane. There's so much wrong with this situation. I knew we shouldn't have-"

"Knew we shouldn't have what?" Terrence asked as he gave Tamara his undivided attention.

Tamara didn't see anger when he asked the question. She saw genuine curiosity. Both of them had been flying since they were kids and neither of them had ever experienced something so tragic while in the air. They were literally trapped in the air with a possible killer. The idea of that didn't sit well with either of them.

"Terrence, I need to tell you something," Tamara said as she tried to still the tremble in her voice.

She had vowed never to tell another living soul about her abilities. But that was before Maahes Air turned into Dead Air.

"Babe, what is it?"

"What I'm about to say may sound crazy, but I can assure you that I'm telling the truth,"

Terrence raised an eyebrow and cocked his head to the side. He wasn't going to say anything, and Tamara knew he wouldn't. When he was intrigued, he simply listened.

"When I was a kid, my mother told me that the women in her family were blessed with a gift and curse called seeing. In our culture, we call it a veil, which means-"

"I know what it means Tee. It means you're supernaturally gifted with a second sight and you have the gift to see things that other people may not be able to predict. Or at least that's the superstition I heard as a kid. So, is that why you didn't want to take the flight? If I knew this beforehand, we would've stayed our black asses home," Terrence admitted.

Tamara was shocked. She had expected him to act like Julius did back when they were a couple. She hadn't expected him to be so nonchalant.

"You tend to forget, that I spent my first six years of life in Georgia. I am a country boy. So, what do you think will happen next?"

Before Tamara could start her sentence, screams erupted from the front of the plane.

"HELP! She's convulsing!!!"

Tamara craned her neck, trying to see what was going on a few rows up. There was too much commotion. A woman was screaming. Flight attendants were huddling around and the doctor from before was approaching.

"We shouldn't have gotten on this plane," Tamara said lowly.

"I wish you would've trusted me with what you were thinking before we left."

Tamara looked at him apologetically. He was right. But she was afraid of his rejection.

"Tell me everything," Terrence commanded.

# CHAPTER 8

The Doctor hopped out of her seat as soon as she heard the scream. But there was nothing she could do. It was the flight attendant this time, Gina. She seemed to have had the same fate as Harold. Shania watched Dr. Adams kneel next to the body, peering up at her with fear in her eyes. She shook her head, confirming something that didn't need confirmation. She was gone.

Shania's brain started moving a mile a minute. Was this targeted or random? Was the flight attendant just collateral damage? She did serve the drink. If it was random, what else is poisoned? How did they get poisoned? If only there were a way to test. Then, a light bulb went off.

"Doctor, do you happen to have any iron supplements on you?"

"I don't," the doctor responded with a confused look on her face.

Shania looked at the other flight attendant, who appeared to be barely holding it together.

Grabbing her by the shoulders, she looked into her eyes.

"Take a few deep breaths for me. I need you to be calm."

"How can I be? Any one of us can be next," she stated shakily.

Shania began taking deep breaths slowly and visibly heaving while looking in the flight attendant's eyes, hoping the attendant would match her actions.

"What's your name?"

"Mariah."

"Ok. Mariah. I have a way to make sure we know if there's any other poison. But I need you to be calm. Can you do that?"

Mariah mimicked Shania's breaths as she nodded her head.

~~~

Shania was now seated, casually watching everyone in the seats ahead of her. She was looking for a sign. Any sign of who might be behind this. They hadn't been in the air for a good hour and there were two bodies to account for. As best they could, they tried to keep a lid on things. The last thing they needed was for the passengers to panic. But when the second body dropped, it was inevitable.

She remembered each face she looked into on her way back to her seat. The Marshal stood guard outside of the cockpit. While Mariah began her announcement.

*Bling, Bom, Boop*

*"Attention passenger."*

The chatter and grumbling that had been the low hum throughout quieted.

*"I know you all have a lot of questions. Just know, we have law enforcement on board. They are doing whatever they can to make sure we are all safe. And the pilot is navigating this storm to make sure we all land safely. I can't give you any answers right now, but we need your help. If anyone is traveling with iron supplements, please hit your call light and I'll come speak with you. The fastened seatbelt sign is still on, let's be sure everyone remains seated. We have two hours and thirty-seven minutes until we touch down."*

Shania saw heads turning. Passengers speaking in whispers. But they weren't the ones that stood out. It was the few that had no reaction, the woman that seemed to be obsessively staring at another. The dude a few rows up laughing and cracking jokes. She noted all the not so typical reactions. Those were the ones that were important. And though she couldn't see all their faces, she noticed the body language.

She saw a few call lights go on. While watching the people that were watching the flight attendant, Shania took a few notes. Just jotting down aisle numbers, seats of people she wanted to pay closer attention to. She didn't know what was going on, but she was going to do her best to find out. Whoever was doing this had no idea, they weren't the only killers on this plane.

"Here you go," Mariah said.

She placed two bottles of iron supplements on the tray in front of Shania. One over the counter, the other prescription.

"Thanks. This will be done in a second."

Shaina poured the pills onto the tray using the bottom of one of the bottles to crush them as finely as she could manage. She scraped the granules into the over-the-counter bottle then filled it halfway with water. After she placed the cap and began shaking the bottle, she turned to Mariah.

"We can use drops of this to detect Cyanide. The iron reacts and the agent will turn blue."

Mariah nodded in understanding.

"Just dab a bit on the things in the galley. Water bottles, handles, food, the rims of cans are all likely places to check. Don't forget the cups."

*Thirty minutes later...*

"What did we come up with?"

Shania stood at the galley entrance waiting for Mariah's response. Water bottles were spread across the small space in front of her and there were piles of containers spread around her feet in disarray. It wasn't the safest considering all the turbulence that seemed determined to stick with them.

"I put all these here," she handed Shania a garbage bag. "Everything else is safe. I still have a few more things to test."

After peering into the garbage bag which contained mostly small alcohol bottles, a few cups and one of the water bottles, Shania nodded. She moved to speak with Thompson.

"We good?" He asked.

"I think we're good with the food area. It's hard to say if this was the distribution or if it's just transference."

"What's next?"

"I-"

"Argggggggh!"

Their conversation was interrupted by screaming further in the cabin. They both rushed down the aisle. By the time they'd gotten to the commotion, other passengers had jumped from their seats. Some were trying to help but they were just in the way.

"Make way," Thompson shouted.

After pushing their way through, the crowd opened to a grizzly sight.

"Everyone to your seats. Now!"

Thompson had pulled his badge from his pocket, holding it in the air. His voice was boisterous and it seemed the baritone had dropped several octaves.

Shania digested the scene one thing at a time.

Blood.

Knife.

Chest.

Face.

Panic.

"What happened here?" Shania questioned.

"Fuck!" The man yelled.

"She stabbed him."

The passenger seated behind Julius pointed to the woman who still stood at the end of the aisle. Her face was expressionless.

Franessa stood at the back galley of the plane. All the time she'd spent staring at the woman Julius had been talking to fueled her hurt, rage. She couldn't get Julius out of her mind. And though she wanted to blame the woman, it was he who had caused her pain. She needed to speak with him. She'd gotten up as if she was going to the bathroom. When she got next to Julius she stopped.

"I miss you and still love you," she told him.

She imagined he would profess he'd felt the same and that he was sorry for ever leaving her. But instead, he laughed.

"Love me? I don't care. I never loved your crazy ass."

The hearts in her eyes turned into flames. She retrieved the ceramic knife that she always smuggled aboard from her back pocket and stabbed him right in the heart like he'd just done to her.

"Nessa?"

Mariah's eyes looked double their size and her jaw hung laxed as she stared at the woman standing a few feet away.

Shania wasn't sure who to focus on, the woman or the bleeding man. Thompson started toward the woman, determined to apprehend her.

"I can't believe that bitch stabbed me," Julius exclaimed.

His breathing was labored. He moved his hand to the handle of the small knife protruding from his chest.

"No! Don't pull it out," Shania instructed.

Julius looked up at her as if she were insane.

"Fuck what you're talking about."

Before she could stop him, he pulled the knife from his body and a stream of blood sailed through the cabin as if it was from the spout of a water fountain. Before landing two rows up, speckles of blood sprinkled the seats, floor and faces of people in its path.

The cabin erupted in chaos. Passengers screaming, crying, frantic. And just when things didn't need to get any more chaotic, there was another flash of lightning followed by a shift in atmosphere. The plane jostled, descended, corrected. Everyone that had not been in their seat belts as they should've been, went airborne.

# CHAPTER 9

After pulling herself up from the floor, it took Shania a few seconds to gather her thoughts. It was the sputter of warm liquid across her face that brought her back to reality. She quickly pulled herself up from the floor, ready to jump to the bleeding man's aid. But when she righted herself, she took in his slumped shoulders, limp arms that hung at his side. There was no rise and fall of his chest nor rasp of breath. Placing her fingers at his wrist, she tried to pace his pulse; there was none.

*Bling, Bom, Boop*

*"I apologize, folks. It looks like this storm is a little more than we anticipated. We will be trying to climb above it, which may add to our flight time. But rest assured, we're going to get you there. Please remain calm and keep those seatbelts fastened."*

Shania wished she could've told him to read the room. Her eyes met with Mariah's as she tried to pull herself up from the floor then quickly fell back to her butt.

"Are you ok?"

"My ankle, I think it's broken."

Shania helped her up then into an empty seat. She scanned the aisle ahead and behind where she stood. The Doctor was on her face about halfway up the aisle towards the front of the plane. She wasn't moving, it was hard to tell if she was breathing with the sway of the plane. Thompson was on his back at the very back of the plane, he wasn't moving. The woman he was headed to apprehend was nowhere in sight.

"I'll be right back. I'm going to check on the others," she told Mariah.

First up was the doctor, she was breathing but unconscious. Then Thompson, he wasn't so lucky. As she got closer, Shania could tell from the position of his head, his neck was broken. Standing over him, his eyes were open her but there was nothing in them. She checked for a pulse, anyway, nothing.

Stepping over him, she made her way back to the galley. She searched the compartments for a first aid kit. Shania picked up a few things and was about to head back up front. As she was heading back, she noticed the panel with the telephone. Picking it up, she placed the handset on her ear. It began to ring.

"Yeah."

"Uh… Who am I speaking with?"

"David Klasky, the co-pilot. How may I help you?"

"David, we're in a dire situation back here."

"Where's Officer Thompson?"

"Dead."

"Excuse me?"

"Dead. This plane needs to land."

"Put one of the flight crew on."

Shania felt a familiar tinge begin to creep up her spine. She wasn't all too pleased with his tone. It was laced with condescension.

"That's not as simple as it sounds. Mariah may have broken her ankle and well, Gina is dead too."

The line was silent for enough seconds for her to wonder if he'd hung up. She heard muffled voices.

"We're going to contact flight control. I'll call you back."

He disconnected before she could respond.

She took the first aid kit then headed back up the aisle.

"Mariah, I'm going to secure your ankle. It's gonna hurt. Take this."

She handed her two bottles of vodka. Mariah wasted no time downing both little bottles.

"Take a deep breath."

Mariah filled her lungs and just as she was exhaling, Shania cinched the gauze she was using to secure her ankle.

"Fuuuuuuuuuuuuuuck!"

"Here," Shania said, handing her another bottle of vodka. "I'm sure someone has some pain meds. I'll see what I can get you."

She stood, taking in the scene, she wasn't sure which action to take next. The doctor still hadn't come to. Passengers were buzzing with panic. Blood was coating the floor. Thompson was too big for her to move alone. *Where did that woman go?*

"Mariah, the woman that did this," she nodded toward the blood on the floor. "Where did she go? Did you see her? Do you know what passenger it was?"

The way she averted her eyes let Shania know she had answers.

"Look. It's people dropping dead. I don't have time for whatever you're thinking about."

Shania's face was blank of expression save her raised eyebrows.

"It was Nessa. She probably went into the belly."

"Did she know him?"

"I-I-I don't know." She hesitated. "She's the pilot's wife."

Shania's eyes bucked.

"I'll be back. You need something more than the painkiller in that case. Maybe the doc has something stronger or one of the other passengers."

When she looked up to go to the front of the cabin, Shania saw Nessa standing in the front galley. Their eyes met just before Nessa knocked on the cockpit door. Shania moved as quickly as she could through the wobbly plane, grabbing seat backs for balance. She could see Nessa's knocks become frantic. All she could do was pray they wouldn't open that door before she got there. Her prayers were unanswered.

"Fran, what's going on?"

David stood with the door ajar, blocking her from entry. Franessa shoved him. He was knocked off balance because he was caught off guard. She moved into the cockpit, closed the door and locked it before he had time to react. All while Shania watched.

"What are you doing?" Carlos questioned.

"What in the hell is going on?"

"People are dropping dead left and right. You just want to leave me out there with them. What kind of husband does that?"

Carlos took an exasperated breath.

"We were just on with flight control. They won't divert us."

*Ring... Ring...Ring*

The cockpit phone rang.

"Don't answer that," Franessa demanded.

*Ring... Ring...Ring*

"Why not?" David gave her a look of confusion.

"It could be the killer."

*Ring... Ring...Ring*

"Even more reason to answer. Let's see what they want."

"It doesn't matter what they want."

The ringing stopped. David stood next to the panel staring at Franessa. She stared back with a defiant look.

"Are you just going to let him ignore my warning?"

She spoke to Carlos but didn't look his way.

*Ring... Ring*

David snatched the phone up before it completed its full cycle.

"Hel-"

His greeting was cut short.

~~~

"David, that woman stabbed a man." Shania listened for his response. "David?"

She pulled the receiver from her ear and looked at it as if it would give her answers.

"Hello?"

There was a gurgle, shuffling then what sounded like the phone being returned to the cradle. She hung up on her end then immediately picked it up to ring again.

*Buzz...Buzz...Buzz...*

The line was busy.

~~~

David stood blinking, unable to speak. The look of surprise was plastered across his face. Franessa watched as he dropped the receiver grabbing his throat. He struggled to breathe as the blood began to coat his fingers and white uniform shirt. When she moved to place the receiver on the cradle, Carlos got the full picture.

"What the fuck did you do?"

His words startled her. She'd forgotten he was there.

Carlos hit the autopilot. He was out of his seat in no time, attempting to save David. It was to no avail. He watched the light go out of his eyes as he slumped to the floor.

"He…"

She couldn't think of the right lie to tell.

"Franessa! What did you do?"

He questioned, looking up at her from his crouched position next to dead David. That's when he noticed the razor blade. It was clutched in the hand that hung at her side.

Her body swayed side to side as she bounced the deadly weapon against her thigh. She wasn't looking at him; she was looking through him.

"He was going to-"

"Answer the phone," he cut her off.

"Talk to that woman. She did all that out there."

"What woman?"

"I don't know who she is."

"You mean…"

**Bang…Bang…Bang…**

The knocking on the cabin door interrupted his question.

"Don't open that!"

# CHAPTER 10

Shania's knuckles pounded the cockpit door with a force that surprised even her.

"Carlos! Open the door. She's not well. I think she just killed the co-pilot! Carlos!!" Shania screamed but received no answer.

Inside the cockpit, Carlos was frozen. He could hear the pounding on the door and he heard the words. He saw what his wife did, but still, he couldn't believe it.

He knew that Franessa was erratic at times. He knew that she was obsessive. Even though she was weighing him down mentally, he made excuses for her behavior. Carlos told himself that Franessa was simply a jealous wife. He never expected her to do what she just did.

It didn't make sense, mainly because Franessa was prissy and high-maintenance. He'd seen her go ape shit when blood got on her fingers while bathing during her menstrual cycle. He couldn't understand how she managed to slit David's throat with ease. Nor could he understand how she managed to smuggle a razor blade aboard. None of this made sense, but he had no choice but to acknowledge the blood pooling around David's lifeless body, and he also had to acknowledge that, as Franessa stood beside David's dead body, she seemed proud.

"Franessa, what-"

"You're not opening that door," Franessa interrupted flatly.

Carlos felt like the cabin was closing in on him. Before this happened, he couldn't deny that he was drained and tired, now he was wide awake. His hands trembled. He was unsure of whether to reach for the communication system or disarm his wife.

"Franessa… this isn't you."

"This is the real me," Franessa whispered, "The one who gets left. The one who watches men throw her away for newer saner bitches. You were supposed to be different."

"Newer saner bitches? What the fuck are you talking about Franessa?"

Carlos was mortified. For the first time since being married, he was truly afraid of her. He had flown planes during storms so severe that he had been nicknamed Zeus. Heavy rain, thunder, and lightning did not bother him at all. But at this very moment, he was locked in a cockpit with a version of his wife that he had not known even existed.

"Franessa, I-"

A loud BANG on the cockpit door interrupted what Carlos was about to say.

"Open this damn door before she kills you too!" Shania shouted.

Franessa turned slowly, her eyes empty but glinting.

"Carlos, don't you dare let that bitch in here. If you do, I'll make sure you regret it."

In the cabin, panic had everyone in a chokehold. Passengers whispered loudly about poison, knives, turbulence, and now a locked cockpit.

Tamara gripped Terrence's hand tightly, her watery eyes shiny with unshed tears. She wanted to be mad at Terrence for buying the tickets in the first place, but she couldn't be. He had only done what any good man would do, surprised her with a trip, like he had hundreds of times before. No, she couldn't be mad at him. She was mad at herself. Her visions had never steered her wrong. Now, because she hadn't listened to the gift that her mother had blessed her with, she was sure none of them would make it off this plane alive.

Terrence could feel Tamara trembling. He wanted to hold her, but he knew that they needed to remain seated.

"Tee? Baby, talk to me. Tell me how you're feeling?"

"We really shouldn't have gotten on this flight. I keep seeing three more,"

Terrence blinked.

"Three more what?"

She turned to meet his gaze, heavy tears finally rolling down her face.

"Three more people to die,"

Terrence leaned closer.

"Are you saying someone else is going to kill again? Why? What do these people have in common? None of this makes any sense Tee," Terrence whispered.

Tamara could hear the fear that he tried so hard to hide. The thing is, she couldn't answer that. She had no idea why any of this was happening.

"I wish I knew why this was happening, but I don't."

**Back in the cockpit...**

Carlos knew time was thinning. His hand inched toward the emergency handset. If he could just call control, they might be able to override.

"Don't do that. If you do, I'll make sure this plane hits the ocean before we even see land," Franessa's voice was eerily calm. The award-winning smile on her face made Carlos cringe.

"Nessa, baby. I don't know what's going on with you, but whatever it is, we can work this out. You're not thinking clearly. Please, please stop this," he pleaded.

"I'm thinking clearly for the first time in my life," she hissed.

"This isn't just about me. It's about all of them. Julius, the bitch he tried to take in the bathroom, that profiler bitch knocking on the door, and even you. Every last one of you treated me like a sideshow. But when this story hits the news? They'll remember my name."

Carlos stared at her as if she were a mental patient. Nothing that she said made any sense to him, and it wouldn't because Franessa had indeed been a mental patient. She spent years of her life being in and out of psych wards.

Her childhood and teen years had been filled with abuse, neglect, and mental illness. Her looks had gotten her everything that she ever wanted from men, but her erratic and unhinged behavior had run each and every one of them off.

"Franessa, Baby, I don't know what you're talking about. But acting like you're not coming back from this,"

Franessa grinned.

"You don't know what I'm talking about. You think I didn't see all the dick pics that you have in your phone. The ones you sent and received. But somehow, I'm the crazy bitch," Franessa laughed as she looked at the blood on her hands.

"What?" Carlos asked, even more confused. He had never taken any dick pics and he certainly hadn't received any. Franessa had him confused with someone else. But who?

Shania backed away from the door. It was no use. That woman was locked in tight—and Carlos wasn't stopping her.

"Mariah," she said as she reached the galley. "How stable is this plane without a co-pilot?"

Mariah, her ankle now wrapped but clearly in pain, shook her head.

"Carlos is one of the best pilots around. He's seen it all he's literally been flying for twenty years. Bodies on a plane is not anything new to him. He can handle this," Mariah said confidently.

Shania sighed. Even through her pain, she could see that Mariah had complete faith in Carlos. But Shania knew differently.

She had seen the strongest men crack under pressure thanks to her father, the late Caesar Brindle. Their trips on Hwy 725 had taught her how to masterfully annihilate the strength of the strongest man. Her father taught her things that the FBI could never teach her.

"Are you ok?" Mariah asked as she watched the expression on Shania's face change from determined to genuine sadness.

Shania blinked rapidly to rid her eyes of the tears forming. She missed her father tremendously, but she did what had to be done. Clearing her emotions, Shania told Mariah the truth that she may not have been ready for.

"In a normal circumstance, I do not doubt that the pilot could handle things, but this situation is completely different. He's locked in the cockpit with a lunatic that just so happens to be his wife,"

"You're right," Mariah admitted.

She knew from day one that Franessa would ruin Carlos's life. She had seen the drastic change in his demeanor since marrying her. From not smiling as much, looking tired, and simply not ironing his uniform. It was as if Carlos could not see past Franessa's beauty, like everyone else could.

"I swear that bitch is a Siren," Mariah blurted angrily.

"A what?"

"A Siren. In Greek Mythology, Sirens are beautiful creatures that lure men to their deaths with their voices. Imagine thinking you're seeing and hearing a beautiful woman, only to see that she's only half a person. Everyone could see her evilness except Carlos, now we're here," Mariah said as a tear slid down her face. "What do we do now?"

"Now we continue to assume worst-case scenarios since we now know that Franessa is capable of murder. How many more murders is she capable of? If she sabotages controls or if she takes him out, then everyone on this plane is dead. So, we need to find help. We need to know if there's someone on this flight who can fly," Shania blurted.

Mariah's eyes darted toward the cabin. No one on the plane looked as if they had any knowledge of what it took to be a pilot.

"You really think a random passenger can fly a commercial jet?"

"I know what you're thinking but looks can be deceiving. We may not need a pilot, but we do need a plan. We also need to consider that there may be someone else behind the murders. Nothing is off the table," Shania said sternly.

~~~

Tamara shook so violently that Terrence wanted to call for a sedative. Yes, he knew that this situation was a scary one but had no idea what caused this new wave of immense terror all he knew was, he was ready to get the fuck off Flight 725.

# CHAPTER 11

"Tee, baby, what's going on?"

Tamara cried violently. How could she tell him that the visions were clearer now? She could see the faces of the people that would die so clearly. The people who would die—their faces, she knew them.

Julius.

Mariah.

And… herself.

"No," she whispered. "That can't be right. I didn't even want to get on this fucking flight. What did I do? Why is it me?"

Tamara asked frantically as she clutched her chest, trying to slow the acceleration of her heart. Looking behind her, she saw the sheet over Julius's dead body. The sight nearly sent her into cardiac arrest.

"Oh my God! We have to stop the deaths. I don't want to die, Terrence. I don't want to-"

Terrence's heart dropped. He refused to trust this gift.

"Nothing is going to happen to you. Nothing. We need to find out who's behind this. The woman that was staring you down, do you think she's behind this?"

Tamara shook her head. She could see the brokenness and damage within Franessa. She was dangerous, but she was not responsible for everything.

"She's a storm. But someone else is the eye. I can't figure-"

Tamara's speech stopped when she heard a sharp but steady voice coming over the intercom to address the passengers.

*"This is Agent Shania Brindle with the FBI. I need to speak to anyone with any flight training, military, commercial, private—immediately. Please raise your hand or turn on your call light."*

A hush fell.

No one moved. For nearly twenty seconds, the only sound was the dull hum of the engines. Then, one hand of an older man went up.

"I am a retired IP,"

"IP?" Shania questioned.

"Yes, ma'am. Instructor Pilot, for Air Education and Training Command of the United States Air Force, headquartered at Randolph Air Force Base. I retired twelve years ago. Now, I only fly my Cessna for recreation," he offered.

"Thank you, God. Thank you!" Mariah said under her breath.

The muscles in Shania's body instantly relaxed. Though she would not show it, she hadn't been this tightly wound since seeing the head of her mother's murderer in her father's safe. Shania felt a huge relief.

"Sir, thank you for your service to our country. May I ask your name?"

"Lieutenant Peter Roland,"

"Lieutenant, I need you. Please come to the front. I'll brief you on what's going on Sir."

Tamara sat up straight as a board before bending over at the waist and vomiting on the floor. She knew the name Peter Roland. She hadn't heard the name in twenty years, but she still knew it. Peter Roland was the father of Patricia Denise Roland, the woman who murdered her mother.

"Babe, what's wrong?" Terrence asked. Earlier, he was convinced that she was pregnant. Now, he wasn't sure if this was pregnancy sickness or fear.

Tamara told Terrence about her parents, but she never mentioned her father's mistress. She had no need. But now, as she watched Lieutenant Roland walking down the aisle, back straight, and shoulders squared, she couldn't help but wonder if he was behind all of this.

~~~

Inside the cockpit, Franessa was spiraling deeper into madness. She had taken David's seat, her hands hovering over controls that she didn't know what the intended purpose was for.

"I guess I'm flying this plane since David's on permanent vacation," Franessa laughed.

Carlos felt stuck, he couldn't move because there was no one else to fly the plane.

"You don't know how to fly a plane. You barely know how to drive a car, that's why you're always getting speeding tickets and parking violations," Carlos spat back.

"I'll figure it out!"

"No, you won't," Carlos snapped. "You'll get us all killed."

She turned on him, eyes wild.

"Maybe that's the point!"

For a moment, the only sound in the cockpit was the steady click of the autopilot knob and her erratic breathing.

*BOOM!!!*

A jolt of turbulence sent them both rocking. Warning lights flashed. The autopilot disengaged.

"Carlos!"

"Oh Shit! Franessa, get the fuck outta here!" Carlos screamed as he grabbed the yoke. For the first time ever, he lost his cool and exploded.

Franessa burst into tears like a scorned child. She did not know how to thrive without chaos, which is why she always caused it. As sad as it was, hearing Carlos scream at her and seeing the true anger and pure disgust on his face was the only thing that calmed down her insanity.

In the cabin, passengers screamed as the plane dipped. Tamara lurched forward, knocking into the seat in front of her. Her vision swam. For a moment, she wasn't in the sky, she was in a hallway. A hospital hallway. The lights flickered. Four stretchers, each with bodies covered in bloodied sheets.

She saw herself on the fourth stretcher.

"No!" She snapped out of it with a scream.

Terrence caught her before she hit the floor.

"It's already started," Tamara choked out.

~~~

At the front, Shania opened the cockpit access panel. With Peter beside her, she keyed in the override code she got from Mariah.

*Beep. Beep. Beep.*

The flashing red light stunned Shania.

"Wrong code," Peter muttered.

"What the fuck?"

Shania tried entering the code again, the light flashed green. As soon as she opened the door, she saw Carlos still fighting the yoke.

"Unless you're trying to help me fly this plane, get the fuck out of here!" Carlos said through gritted teeth, a vein literally bulging from his temples to the center of his forehead.

Shania burst in, weapon drawn.

"Actually, I did bring you some help. Meet Lieutenant Peter Ronald, Retired Instructor Pilot for AETC. Franessa, step away from the controls!"

Franessa turned, blade in hand, screaming.

"No! You don't get to take him too!"

A shot rang out.

Franessa collapsed.

Carlos stared at the blood pooling under her. Tears filled his eyes. As ill as she was, she was still his wife.

"I'm sorry, Franessa," he said quietly.

"I didn't think I'd ever see things like this after leaving the force. Sorry for your loss," Peter said as he slid into the co-pilot seat.

With Peter as the co-pilot, the plane quickly leveled out. But no one spoke. The silence was unnerving.

Shania returned to the cabin, exhausted but focused. Bodies remained. Blood soaked the aisle. No one dared move or speak unless instructed.

Carlos stayed in the cockpit, hands white-knuckled around the controls. He didn't speak.

Tamara leaned into Terrence.

"Baby, it's over. The next time you say we won't take a flight. I'll listen. I swear to God, I'll listen," Terrence said as he stroked Tamara's hand, but Tamara was unresponsive.

"Tee, Baby-"

"It's not over, Terrence. Think about it. None of this makes sense. The first passengers were poisoned. Why? Who were they and why were they poisoned? Something else is going on here. That lady was not the only threat. She was never the only threat. Someone else is on this flight. Something-"

"What do you mean?"

"I think-"

Blood-curdling screams erupted from the front of the plane, sending terror through the plane once again.

# CHAPTER 12

When the scream came, Shania leaned against the wall of the galley. She closed her eyes, trying to calm her thoughts. It was growing increasingly harder for her to keep that tingling feeling that crept up her spine at bay.

"What now?!"

She took a deep breath before her eyes fluttered open. Her eyes met Mariah's.

Someone else was dead.

Shania didn't need to go investigate. She knew it was poison. Mariah placed a sheet over the man. This took her back to the conversation she was trying to have with Thompson before more hell broke loose.

*How was this poison being administered? Was it targeted or did these people tie together somehow?*

Mariah had hobbled herself to the front galley where Shania stood. She pulled her flight crew seat down and sat.

"Can you get me a flight manifest?"

She nodded, grabbed a handheld device, tapped on the screen then handed it to Shania. No obvious connection jumped out at her. Her mind cycled through a multitude of questions.

"Mariah, how well did you know Gina?"

"We were cool."

"Do you know if she had some sort of connection to Harold?"

Mariah shook her head.

"What about the last victim?"

"Charlie, he's a, he was a frequent flyer. Everyone knew Charlie. He was a good time."

"What do you mean by that?"

"He's a party boy. Anytime you were in the city with him, he made sure everyone had a good time."

"Any of those parties get out of hand?"

Her face wore an expression as if she were thinking about it as she shook it. Then her eyes went wide.

"When I first got hired, there was this older flight attendant, she's retired now."

"Did something happen to her?"

"No. She saw me getting close to Gina and she told me to watch myself around her. When I asked her what she meant, she had a story to tell. I don't know how true it was."

"How did the story go?"

"She told me she'd heard once that Gina was questioned by the police about some woman."

"Questioned, about what?"

"She didn't give me particulars. She just said to watch myself. It was like she didn't want to say."

"Did you ever mention it to Gina?"

Mariah shook her head. "I blew it off. Gina had never done anything questionable."

"So, you and Gina hung out outside of work?"

"We have."

"What about Charlie? You partied with him too?"

"Like I said. Charlie was a good time."

"Were drugs involved?"

Mariah looked away. Shania stared at her in silence until she slowly nodded her head.

"Did Gina indulge?"

Mariah nodded.

"What about Harold? Did Charlie and Harold seem friendly?"

"Not that I noticed."

Shania looked out into the cabin. Her eyes landed on everyone seated.

"And you're sure Harold and what was the girl's name that sat next to him?"

"Clarrisa."

"Are you sure Harold and Clarrisa didn't know each other?"

"No. He told me, they'd just met when he asked if she could switch seats to sit next to him."

"What else did he tell you?"

"Nothing much, he was from Connecticut, he was in financial planning... oh he said he'd won this trip."

"From where?"

"I didn't ask, he didn't say."

Shania sat in her thoughts.

~~~

Terrence finally got Tamara a bit calmer. He kept his tone steady and reassuring. Tee finally agreed to half of a Xanax. It helped her. But Terrence had no clue of the vision that kept flashing in her eyes.

"I'm not sure exactly how your gift works, but what I do know is the future is forever changing. Just because you saw it doesn't mean it won't change."

Tamara held on to that. She resolved that she could change what she saw. It took a few minutes while Terrence held her closely, but her breathing had seemed to fall into its normal pattern. Her mind was clearer and she knew what she needed to do.

She reached up, pressing the call button.

"What are you doing?"

"I know what needs to be done. Don't worry."

~~~

Mariah saw the call light go on and rolled her eyes.

"Why? Just sit there," she said quietly.

"Don't worry. I got it." Shania told her as she went to stand.

When Shania peered at the passenger who pressed the call button, she recalled the woman Franessa had been staring at before she went ape shit. There were questions she had. Hopefully, this passenger had answers.

The weather outside was still dark and ominous, but at least it was a little calmer. Her trek down the aisle didn't garner as much of a stagger.

"How may I help you?"

"You're with the FBI, right?" Tamara questioned.

"Yes. My name is Shania Brindle. Did you know the gentleman that was stabbed? If I recall, there was an exchange between you and him just after takeoff."

Tee cut her eyes toward Terrence, she hadn't told him about the entirety of their exchange. But it didn't matter now, Julius was dead.

"Yeah, Julius was my ex. A narcissistic asshole."

"And the woman?"

"I didn't know her. Never met her. We noticed her staring daggers at me. I put two and two together and figured it had something to do with him. Some tigers never change their stripes."

"Did you know the other gentleman? Harold Potas?"

"No." Tamara shook her head. "But that copilot is familiar to me."

"How?"

"His daughter killed my mother."

"You think he may have something to do with what's happening on this flight?"

"I have no idea."

"Wait. I'm sorry. You're the one who hit the call button. How can I help you?"

"That's just it. I think I can help you."

"How?"

Tamara took a deep breath.

"This is something I've never said out loud to a total stranger. Hell, I just told my fiancé. You might not believe in this kind of thing, but I see things."

"What things?"

"Visions, I have visions, usually in flashes. And I get feelings. Right now, these feelings are telling me-" She stopped midsentence, gazed at Shania then continued. "You're the answer to our prayers."

"Did your visions tell you who is poisoning people?"

"No," Tamara shook her head. "But they showed me, pin holes, needle marks. Does that mean anything?"

"Maybe."

Shania made her way back through the cabin. This time, she stopped at the sheet-covered bodies. By the time she made it back to where Mariah sat, she'd had one thing answered, more questions and a strong suspicion of who caused this.

# CHAPTER 13

"Mariah, how's that ankle?"

"Throbbing."

"I have a plan. We need to figure out who killed these people before this plane lands."

Mariah looked at her watch.

"What do you need me to do?"

"Maybe nothing. Just keep your eyes open."

Shania made her way to the cockpit, stepping over Franessa's body in the process. She had managed to drag her out of the cockpit so that Carlos didn't have to be locked in with his dead wife. Shania knocked on the door, waited a few seconds before the door was opened.

"How much longer do we have?"

"This murder box is on its approach, we should be landing in about 45," Peter answered.

"Ok."

"The authorities will be on the ground when we land. We've been instructed not to pull into a gate."

"Protocol." Shania nodded. "Thanks. See you on the ground."

She stepped away from the door then headed back into the main cabin. Before moving away from Franessa, she checked her wrists, neck, and arms. More answers, more questions.

"Can I ask you a few questions?"

Clarissa looked up at her with a stoic expression.

"Sure."

"Come up front."

"O-Ok," Clarissa said hesitantly.

They made their way to the front of the plane. Mariah was now seated in one of the front row seats.

"Go ahead. Have a seat."

Shania pointed to the seat next to Mariah.

"I don't know what I can help you with. Like I said, I just met Harold."

"You've said that. Did you know any of the other passengers?"

Clarissa's brows creased.

"No."

"Why are you headed to L.A.?"

"I have an audition."

"So, you're an actress? I'm trying to be. I've been a couple independent films."

"What's the name of the film you're auditioning for?"

"Why does it matter? It's not like I'll be able to perform after all this."

"I'm just curious about that."

"It's called No Strings. It's about a dating app and three couples that interact with it."

"How exciting for you."

"I just want to get off this plane."

"We all want that, I think."

"But some of us won't be getting off this plane," she started crying.

Shania wasn't buying her tears.

"You can help me figure out what happened to them."

"How?" Clarissa's face wore more worry than curiosity.

"Sit tight."

Shania walked off while Mariah kept up small talk with Clarissa when she returned, Dr. Adams was with her. They stood in front of Clarissa.

"What are the symptoms you're experiencing?" Dr. Adams asked.

Clarissa looked up at her in confusion.

"What?"

"Ms. Brindle says you're feeling sick. We want to make sure you aren't exposed to the poison. What are you experiencing?"

"What are you talking about? I feel fine."

"What's this about?" Dr. Adams questioned.

"You tell me," Shania responded.

"Look, I don't know what you're talking about."

"But you do. You know I checked the bodies."

"We both did. They were poisoned."

"But how?"

"That's the million-dollar question, isn't it?"

"What if I told you, I found out how the victims were poisoned?"

"So, you figured out who did it?" Mariah asked.

"I'm pretty close."

"That's great, enlighten us," Clarrisa chimed in.

"Would you believe that I found a small pin hole in all of them?"

Shania noticed Clarissa and Dr. Adams exchanged a brief look.

"Where? I didn't notice that."

"That's funny. Because I'm sure you're the one that put them there. At least, the ones Clarrisa here didn't take care of."

"What are you talking about?" Clarissa's voice began to crack, her eyes filled with tears.

"Drop the act. The crying does nothing for me."

There was no more pretending. Shania's patience was wearing thin. Her diplomacy meter was on E. Putting a hole in Franessa's head gave her a bit of release but if the plane didn't land soon, she wasn't sure what would happen.

Clarissa stared at Shania blankly. All the pretense of grief and sadness had disappeared. She twisted her head, rolled her shoulders then sat up straighter.

"Fuck it!"

"Clarissa." Dr. Adams said her name in effort to caution her words.

"It's fine Mom."

Shania looked from Clarissa to the good doctor then back again. She hadn't connected that dot. But it helped fill in the blank or two.

"So, let me tell you what I think. You tell me if I got it right," Shania said.

Clarissa nodded.

"Cool. So, the poisoned people wronged you in some way. You orchestrated all this to get revenge. Mom was here to misdirect the cause of death. But you didn't count on me being on this plane."

"They didn't just wrong me. They killed my sister."

"And where do you come in?" Shania directed her question to Mariah.

"She was my best friend."

"The story you told me about Charlie and Gina was true?"

"She used to work with Gina. Marissa, my sister," Clarrisa explained.

"I remember when she called me whispering into the phone that she needed help. She couldn't tell me where she was. She was high, I could tell from the droll of her voice," Mariah stated.

"When the police found my daughter, she had been raped. They listed her cause of death as an overdose."

"Marissa called me that afternoon when she landed. My sister always let me know where she was when she had an overnighter. It was a thing like where in the world is Marissa. As far as I knew, she hadn't planned on doing anything. Then the next thing I knew, she was gone."

"The police weren't doing anything. So, we hatched our own plan," Clarissa added.

"And you," Shania pointed at Mariah. "Took this job to find out who she was hanging with."

"Yup."

*Bling, Bom, Boop*

*"Great news, folks. The runway is in sight."*

The plane erupted in cheers.

"Thank God!" Shania said.

Before they knew it, the plane was touching down, rolling to a stop on the tarmac.

"I suppose we'll be arrested."

"Dr. Adams, why do you suppose that?"

"You know what we did," Clarissa said.

"But I'm the only one who knows what you did."

"The police will investigate."

"They will. They'll never connect the dots."

"You did."

"But they're lazy. They'll go for the easiest explanation. This will all get blamed on the pilot's wife. She had a psychotic episode. That was your plan, wasn't it Doctor?"

"Her behavior was erratic. She just needed a little push. A cocktail of Prozac, Adderall and methamphetamine did the trick." Doctor Adams shrugged. "I had no idea she had smuggled weapons on board."

"Thompson's dead, no fault of yours. He was the only other person that might suspect a second assailant. Your secret is safe with me."

"Why would you help us?" Mariah questioned.

"Let's just say, I have experience with grief and payback."

"I'm not sure what to say. Thank you?" Dr. Adams said.

"Just stick to your plan. You don't know each other, you don't know what happened."

"I-I-I don't know what to say," Clarissa stammered.

"YOU just turn those tears back on." Shania winked. "Great job, ladies. I couldn't have done a better job if I say so myself."

**Thank You for Reading** *Flight 725*

With gratitude,
**Kaylynn Hunt & Octavia Grant**

We truly appreciate you taking the time to journey with us on *Flight 725*. We hope the twists, turns, and turbulence kept you on the edge of your seat!

If you enjoyed the ride, we would *love* for you to **rate and review** the book on your favorite platform. Your feedback helps other readers discover the story—and it means the world to us.

**Haven't read** *Hwy 725* **yet?**

You're missing the beginning of the journey! Dive into *Hwy 725* to experience Shania's story and discover how it all started. Trust us—you'll want to see where the road first began before the flight took off.

Thanks again for your support. We can't wait to share what's next.

**Octavia Grant** found her passion for Creative Writing in  2002, her Junior year at Georgetown High School (Georgetown, SC). She began writing professionally in 2016, two years later she decided to take the reins of her literary career and became an Independent Author. As an Independent Author, Octavia has penned over 30 novels. She's spoken on the Thrilling Tales Author Panel at ESSENCE Fest, she's been interviewed by Narrator iiKane, interviewed by Literary Reviewer and Movie Commentator Tamara Walker of Tam Telling Tales, featured in magazines WYB Lifestyle, VoyageJacksonville, Canvas Rebel, Bold Journey and named in 160 Black Women In Horror. Octavia's psychological thriller novella, Dear Vicky, was the winner of the Black Girls Who Write Its Lit Award for Best Black Mystery/Suspense, Audio In Black North Star Award Winner, and AAMBC Award Winner for Mystery/Thriller Book of the Year.

Octavia loves reader interaction and encourages her readers to follow her on social media:

FB: Octavia Taneka Grant

IG: Octavia_vs_otaneka

TikTok: Octavia the Author

Twitter: Tavi_vs_otaneka

**Kaylynn Hunt** is a Detroit native with an insatiable passion

for storytelling. A multi-genre author who draws from both imagination and real-life experiences, she creates bold, emotionally rich stories that challenge convention and pull readers in from the first page. Her love for writing began early, and over time, her passion expanded to screenwriting as she began adapting her books for the screen.

Known for her unconditional love and loyalty, Kaylynn treats friends like family and believes in living and writing outside the box. Whether on the page or the screen, her work delivers thought-provoking journeys designed to stir emotions and spark conversation. She hopes to inspire others to dream boldly, think deeply, and never stop growing.

Connect with her on all platforms: @Kaylynn Hunt